To: Christie
From: Grandad

S0-AWM-408

'97

The Christmas Pony

Helen McCully & Dorothy Crayder

with illustrations by
Robert J. Lee

NIMBUS
PUBLISHING LTD

To the memory of
Herbert Read & Ethel Lowerison
McCully

Copyright © 1997 Wayne Barchart in trust

All rights reserved. No part of this book covered
by the copyrights hereon may be reproduced or used
in any form or by any means—graphic, electronic,
or mechanical—without the prior written permission
of the publisher. Any request for photocopying,
recording, taping, or information storage and
retrieval systems of any part of this book shall be
directed in writing to the Canadian Reprography
Collective, 379 Adelaide Street West, Suite M1,
Toronto, Ontario M5V 1S5.

Nimbus Publishing Limited
PO Box 9301, Station A
Halifax, NS B3K 5N5
(902) 455-4286

Facsimile of the 1967 edition
Illustrations: Robert J. Lee
Design: Arthur B. Carter, Halifax
Published in agreement with Wayne Barchart
Printed and bound in Hong Kong

Canadian Cataloguing in Publication Data

McCully, Helen.
The Christmas pony
(Nimbus classics)
ISBN 1-55109-212-3

1. Ponies—Juvenile fiction. 2. Christmas stories.
I. Crayder, Dorothy. II. Lee, Robert J., 1921-
III. Title. IV. Series.

PS8575.C85C47 1997   JC813'.54   C97-950026-5
PZ7.M13915Ch 1997

Chapter One

"Every child should have a pony."

People are always saying things like that. Some mean what they say, some don't; and some who mean it are forgetful. Getting a pony is chancy.

Mrs. McCully meant what she said and would remember it, in itself an historical fact worth recording. (Most of what is to be recorded here will be fact, and what will not be fact will be the truth as it is remembered by a quirky memory.)

Sitting in the breakfast room of her Victorian house in Amherst, Nova Scotia, Mrs. McCully spoke these words two years before the big guns went off in August of 1914.

"Every child should have a pony."

Mrs. McCully repeated this because Dr. McCully seemed not to have heard her the first time. He was busy eating a kipper.

"So he should," said Dr. McCully.

"But I mean it, Herb."

"Of course you do. Who said you didn't?"

"Well, you don't sound as if you do."

"Do what?"

"Mean it."

"It's dangerous to sound convincing while eating a kipper. All those bones. Just take my word for it, won't you?"

Mrs. McCully sighed. Dr. McCully ate a kipper every single morning for breakfast, which made conversation rather one-sided.

"Well then," she said, "it's settled."

"Good," said Dr. McCully, who liked things to be settled quickly.

"The children will be enchanted," said Mrs. McCully.

"What children?" asked Dr. McCully.

"Our children," Mrs. McCully said conversationally. "All three of them. Surely you remember them? Your very own children?"

Dr. McCully put down his knife and fork and gave Mrs. McCully his full attention at last.

"Ethel McCully," he asked, "what in heaven's name are you up to now?"

"A pony for our children for Christmas." Mrs. McCully gave her husband her very best smile, the one she reserved for special requests.

"Are you crazy?" he asked.

"But you agreed with me, Herb."

"In theory, only in theory. Ponies are for rich people, which we are not." Dr. McCully went back to his kipper.

The McCullys may not have been rich, but they certainly lived as if they were. This is a lovely way to live; much more agreeable than living as if you are poor when you're rich. But it's only a lovely way to live if you can do it. Not everyone can; moreover, not everyone should. Just as not everyone should climb Mount Everest or sail across the Pacific on a raft.

The McCullys were very good at living as if they were rich.

They were also very good at making Amherst an attractive place to live. This was not easy. "Busy Amherst" as it was called was a factory town. It had wood works and woolen works, and manufactured railroad cars, engines, and caskets. All worthy and useful occupations, but it is more attractive to live where they are not.

The McCullys lived where the pavement ended, beyond Morse's Corner, on land that was meadow, orchard, and garden. Beneath them lay the Tantramar Marshes, a great swamp from the head of the Bay of Fundy, famous for its tidal tricks, to Northumberland Strait. Between the strait and the open sea, north northeast, are Prince Edward Island, the Magdalen Islands, Newfoundland—north, cold, and discouraging for gardens. But the McCullys had a charming garden, all the more exciting for having been painstakingly coaxed into existence by Mrs. McCully, flower by flower.

When the first pink flower showed on the japonica by the garden wall, she would call out to Helen, the middle child. Mrs. McCully and Helen were the ones who loved the garden and the house best. Consequently, Helen became her mother's favorite, which made the other children jealous. But Helen thought it only fair for her to be the favorite because Nora was the one who had the curls and Richard was a boy, which was almost as good. (In those days, before such complications as sibling rivalry had been invented, it was considered only natural to have favorite children.)

"Helen!" Mrs. McCully would call from the garden.

Helen would leap from bed, fly down the winding staircase with its mahogany banister, and out through the breakfast room into the garden. No matter that she had been awakened from a sound sleep. There would be a tiny shock as her bare feet first touched the cold dew and then the hem of her nightgown would be wet around her ankles. No matter; she knew that the first bud of something had opened during the night and that it would be worth seeing, worth remembering forever.

Mrs. McCully had been born in the house they lived in. Her father, a sea captain, had built it in 1860, a good year for Victorian houses, one more inclined toward the simple elegance of the eighteenth century than the gewgaws of the nineteenth.

Captain Richard Lowerison had owned into the Dorchester fleet and had retired in 1850 when he was thirty-nine years old with one hundred thousand dollars. In those days, this nice round figure with only six digits entitled a man to be called rich. But the captain had been a stubborn man and he had kept his money in sail, when ships were going to steam.

In the nick of time, however, while he still had the money, he built his house. He built it on a terraced slope and he built it for keeps. It was large and square and its clapboard had been painted a pale yellow and its trim white. (Later, when the first motors raised too much dust on the road, it was painted a dark red.) Its façcade billowed gently with bay windows from which one could look down on miles and miles of marsh.

The interior was as serene as the exterior, its serenity quite impervious to the raging storms of Nova Scotia and the fun-loving, salty-tongued, high-tempered McCullys. Big airy rooms with high ceilings opened off a wide central hall, on whose walls an itinerant artist had painted a seascape, a schooner running with bare poles from an approaching squall. Drifting up the winding stairway, throughout the house, mingling with the scents of waxes and polishes on the floors and furniture and quince and potpourri in the drawers and closets, was the smell of salt and sea from the marsh. The McCullys were never far from their beginnings.

The house had about twenty rooms, give or take a dressing room or a nook or other oddment, a sensible number if you consider that families were expected to be large and one never knew when it might not have to include an aging, or ailing, or somewhat impoverished,

grandparent or other relative unto the third or fourth cousin. It certainly had to have spare rooms for guests who came to dinner parties and dances or just to visit for a couple of weeks. And a dressing room for Mrs. McCully. And a sewing room. And a library. And rooms for the servants; the servants being Susan, the cook, who had come to work for the captain and his wife when she was twelve years old, and Annie, the "inside girl." Laurent, the French Canadian jack of all trades, lived in the little caretaker's house.

But the rooms that really counted were the Big Rooms. They were where the parties and the dances took place. They were where Christmas took place (along with the dining room, of course). They were where Santa Claus came. He came down from the north, traveled swiftly over the marsh, slid down the chimney, and landed in the Big Rooms. It would have been a long cold journey with high winds, and Mrs. McCully always left a glass of milk and a doughnut for him. But being a busy man in that season, he always rushed off leaving part of the milk and part of the doughnut uneaten. And from his trip down the chimney, some soot marks on the glass.

The Big Rooms were very big indeed and very lovely. They were two rooms which opened into each other with folding doors, and since each had its own fireplace and marble mantel, when they were in use two fires glowed at the same time in their Victorian grates. (All over the house there were Victorian grates in constant use.) The floors were covered with Brussels carpets and the windows with Brussels lace curtains and across the top of the windows brass lambrequins were kept in high polish by Laurent. The walls had been papered a pale blue with gold fleurs-de-lis. When the McCullys had their dances—which was as often as possible—huge sheets of linen were stretched over the carpets, hooked on at the sides, and waxed over for dancing.

Sometime around the turn of the century a verandah had been

stuck on the house; architecturally this had been considered vandalism. It opened off the Big Rooms with French doors and was rarely used, but the Christmas we are remembering it justified its existence.

The captain had also built himself an icehouse, a big barn, the caretaker's house, and a carriage house with a special feature—a home freezer circa 1860.

A double-walled room had been built in the carriage house; insulated with sawdust and filled with hay, it was a place where every winter a flock of birds was stored. The term flock is not used casually; it was quite literally a flock. Ducks, chickens, geese, turkeys, whatever; the total output of Mr. Brooks's poultry farm. Mr. Brooks would arrive with his flock and be met by Mrs. McCully and Laurent. Mrs. McCully would inquire of Mr. Brooks what species of bird he had brought this time. Then Mrs. McCully would telephone a market in Amherst to find out what the going price was that day for that particular bird. The price thus fixed without argument, the birds would be weighed on the big scale kept in the pantry, and Mrs. McCully's business with Mr. Brooks would be concluded. Laurent would now take over: he would hang the birds in the woodhouse, where the freezing temperature of Nova Scotia would do the rest. When the birds were frozen, they were wrapped in newspaper and laid down in the freezing room.

What with a flock of birds on hand and oysters bought by the barrel, the McCullys were always ready for guests. "We eat up all our money," Dr. McCully was fond of saying. "I know," Mrs. McCully would reply, "but it tastes so good. Don't you agree?" And Dr. McCully would have to agree that it did.

Helen, the child who loved the house best, loved it as if it were a person. Walking home from school in the late afternoon, she watched for the first glimpse of smoke spiraling from the many pinkish brick chimneys. When she saw it, she felt as if the house had arms reaching out to welcome her. Always at this moment she would begin to run toward them.

But of all the things that this house was, it was a house that had been made for Christmas.

In such a house, one did not suddenly stub one's toe on Christmas and frantically rush about preparing for it at the last minute, as if it were a disaster. In such a house, the whole year was tilted toward Christmas, so it was only natural for Mrs. McCully to have had ponies on her mind that windy September morning.

She left the breakfast room and met Dr. McCully's mother in the hall. Dr. McCully's mother was a very strict Baptist and she had had her breakfast much earlier. (Mrs. McCully, who was Church of England, as were the children, loved to do all the things her mother-in-law considered sinful; she loved to play cards and dance and drink; Dr. McCully enjoyed these things too, but he was agnostic. Whenever there was any money to give, however, he gave it to the Church of England for the sake of his wife and children, which rather displeased his mother.)

"The children are going to have a pony for Christmas," young Mrs. McCully announced to her mother-in-law.

Her mother-in-law frowned. "A pony? You mean a hobby-horse, don't you?"

"I mean a pony. A real live pony."

Dr. McCully's mother was endowed with the ability to express maximum disapproval with minimum words. This sometimes gave her the appearance of a person who was smelling something unpleasant.

"A pony? Whatever for? Does Herb know about this?"

Mrs. McCully chose not to answer. She hurried on her way. Since Santa Claus could scarcely bring a pony down the chimney, she would have to arrange things herself. It was not going to be simple and she had no time to lose.

Chapter Two

Hurrying on her way, Mrs. McCully came close to tripping over the Newfoundland, Max, and the parrot. Mrs. McCully had become the surprised owner of the parrot at a white elephant sale for the Daughters of the British Empire. Being herself a D.B.E., she had naturally wanted the parrot to bring as high a price as possible; to this end, she had been a prime mover in raising the bids, confident that a true lover of parrots would pay a good price to own one. Unfortunately, her bid remained the highest and she came home with the bird. Amazed as everyone was at this unexpected addition to the McCully household, nothing was more amazing than Dr. McCully's reaction to it. Instead of hitting the roof, he rather sheepishly said, "I have always wanted to own a parrot." But this sentiment had no effect upon the parrot; the parrot bit the doctor, just as he did everyone else.

The parrot was strolling down the long hall toward the Big Rooms, taking his own sweet time as was his custom, and the dog followed him, keeping his distance respectfully as was *his* custom. This parade took place every morning. Every morning, Max, a big black retriever with soft brown eyes and soft ways, sat on his haunches in front of the parrot's cage in the breakfast room and waited with his nose twitching and his eyes glued to the bird. Waiting in front of the cage, Max looked anything but soft. However, when the parrot decided it was time to fly out of the cage, Max stood back politely and allowed the parrot to settle on the floor and precede him down the hall. The McCullys took this parade quite for granted.

But this morning, Mrs. McCully, having had a sudden brainstorm, turned back and collided with the parrot just as he was about to enter the Big Rooms. The parrot let out an enraged squawk and tried to bite her ankle and Max yipped his sympathy with the parrot.

"Sh-h-h!" Mrs. McCully scolded. "You'll wake the children."

The parrot regained his composure and headed for his favorite perch on the wood box in front of the fireplace. Max stretched out, couchant, at the parrot's feet and gazed at him with his doleful eyes.

Actually, Mrs. McCully was not one to consider children's sleep a matter of life or death; life was too full of too many wonders for them to sleep it away. But this particular Saturday morning, she wanted to be free to plan; she didn't want them at her heels.

She stepped into the Big Rooms and stood still. The doors were still folded back from the last party and the great interior was shimmering with sunlight and shadow, like watered silk. Everything was in beautiful order. Laurent, who rose at four thirty in the morning to tend the furnace and the fires, had already been there to polish brass and whatever else was polishable, Saturday morning being polishing morning.

The McCully household was run by Susan and Laurent and Annie as if the old sea captain were in charge. Beginning at six o'clock sharp on Monday morning, the washing machine was wheeled into the kitchen and was cranked all morning, churning

away at the Irish linens and the muslins and the cambrics and the
ginghams of the McCullys; while the big copper boiler whitened all
that was intended to be white and sometimes, in the general frenzy,
that which was not. On Tuesday the big flatirons—and the little ones
imported from France for ruffles and pleats—were kept hot on the
big black iron stove, and so on into the week, each hour of the day
was logged.

Mrs. McCully, who knew perfectly well that her house was in
order, was not in the Big Rooms to hunt dirt. She was there for
dreaming and scheming.

"What are you smiling at?"

Helen, in her nightgown, had arrived.

"Why aren't you asleep?" her mother asked irritably.

Helen accepted her mother's inconsistencies.

"I heard Max yipping and I wanted to see what was up. What is
up? Are you having another dance again?"

Helen adored the dances; she always sat on the stairs and
watched them, sometimes falling asleep in the process. The most
ordinary of her parents' friends, even those who were fat and clumsy,
were ravishingly transformed into royalty as they waltzed on the
linen-covered carpet.

Mrs. McCully, who hadn't thought of having a dance quite so
soon again, decided she would. Not that she was opposed to an
absolutely essential white lie, but why not replace it with an amusing
truth?

"Yes," she said, "yes, I am going to have another dance. And
now that you know that, would you consider getting dressed?"

"Before Christmas? Another dance before Christmas?"

Mrs. McCully jumped. Sometimes it seemed as if this middle
child of hers was too close to her, practically inside her mind.

"Christmas? Who's thinking about Christmas in September?"

"I am," said Helen, who always spoke her mind.

"Oh, do go upstairs and take your bath. You'll miss your turn if you're not careful."

Helen, hoping that she had missed her turn, went upstairs wondering what her mother was keeping from her. "Christmas in September?" Since when was there a season for thinking about Christmas? No, something was up. Something big.

Mrs. McCully went back to dreaming and scheming and had just stepped through the French doors and out onto the verandah when she heard a bloodcurdling scream.

She raced to the foot of the stairs in the hall and Max and the parrot flew up them.

"What happened?" she shouted.

Susan came running from the kitchen where she was baking bread, and Annie from the pantry where she was polishing silver, and old Mrs. McCully from her room where she was reading Job, her favorite book in the Bible.

"Dad-dy!"

It was Helen who was screaming.

Dr. McCully, who never allowed anything to interfere with his reading of the Amherst *Daily News* and the Halifax *News Chronicle*, and who was accustomed to shouts and screams, did not come out of the library.

"Herb!" Mrs. McCully shouted. "The child may be dead."

"Then we have the liveliest ghost in Cumberland County." But he came out and joined the shouting. "What in blazes is it?"

" 'Oh that I had given up the ghost.... Are not my days few? cease then and let me alone, that I may take comfort a little ...,' " old Mrs. McCully quoted.

"She's a ninny, a ninny, a skinny ninny," Richard stormed.

Richard, it seemed, was in a position to make such a qualifying judgment, having barged in on Helen in her tub.

"I am not. I'm shy. Everyone knows I'm shy." She was still screaming.

"Am I shy too?" Nora, all curls and innocence, appeared at the top of the stairs. Nora, quite sensibly, enjoyed being the baby of the family.

Everyone—except Helen—had lost interest in this particular storm. The senior Mrs. McCully returned to her room, murmmering, " 'Naked came I out ... and naked shall I return thither....' "

That Saturday morning was not a good one for Helen.

She wasn't talking to anyone. But it was a perfect morning for wandering over the marsh, kicking and snapping at any salt hay that had not been cut down in August.

She went through the apple orchard where Laurent was now gathering Gravensteins. He threw her one and she caught it on the fly, the first decent thing that had happened to her that morning.

"Thanks," she said and bit into the apple streaked with dark red and orange. Even she had to admit it was a perfect one.

Laurent, who was a man of few words, grunted.

Catching the apple, Helen had been tempted to smile, but since the best way to enjoy the marsh was to be unhappy, she was determined to remain so.

The McCullys owned a piece of the Tantramar Marshes. The old French settlers were said to have named the marshes "Tintamarre," meaning loud noise, because of the crying and the flapping of the wings of the wild fowl who came there in the spring and the autumn.

The marsh was not only marvelous for unhappiness, but also a place of other delights. Haying in August, gathering in the first weeks of September the wild salt-marsh mushrooms (baskets of them that Susan cooked in sweet cream and served on toasted homemade bread); skating, and driving over its ice in a sleigh in the winter, the marsh was a place for all seasons.

The wind had become fitful, sweeping blue-white clouds over a pale blue sky and over the sun, making it blink on and off like the blinker on a buoy. And where some hay had been left standing, the wind made weird reedy music.

"Why do you look so sad?"

A girl named Emma, who lived up the road, had come to join her.

Helen was pleased to see that her sadness had been noticed, but she couldn't think of a reason to give to someone who was not her best friend. (That morning she would have been hard put to come up with a reason even to her best friend.)

"Do you think Santa Claus is lonely?" she asked sadly, having come up with the first sad thought she could think of.

She was to regret bitterly having expressed this sad thought. If only she had kept her mouth shut—but everyone talks too much sometimes and this was one of those times.

"Santa Claus?" Emma asked, imitating a dowager. "Helen McCully, do you mean to tell me that you still believe in Santa Claus?"

Emma was three quarters of a year older than Helen, and she also had been to Boston recently.

A gust of wind whistled through the salt hay and some gulls laughed hysterically.

Helen turned toward the north and the wind made her eyes smart.

"Doesn't everyone?" she asked.

"Of course not, silly."

One word led to another. Their hair was a bit silky for pulling,

but they managed quite well. It turned into the worst fight either one of them had ever had and they both ended up in a ditch.

"You'll see—" Helen sobbed, not because her knee was skinned, but because a great friend had been insulted, "you'll see ... he won't come to your house at all this year ... that'll teach you not to believe in him...."

And it was at that moment that a doubt, a very tiny one, no bigger than a sliver of splinter, stabbed Helen's heart: what if Emma was right? What if there was no longer any Santa Claus?

Out there on the marsh the two girls sobbed and there was a sudden big rush of wind from the north and some more laughter.

You'll see ... you'll see ... the wind whistled through the salt hay....

Chapter Three

The house was quiet. That is, the people and animals in it were quiet; the house itself was noisy, sighing and whispering and creaking and squeaking as if its wood still stood in the forest.

The cats were asleep. They were strewn all over the house—the big tortoise-shell one, who was the undisputed leader, hogging the warmest spot next to the stove in the kitchen, the dainty and lazy Maltese in the breakfast room because it was there she had once caught a dim-witted mouse by merely stretching a paw, the elegant black one in front of the fireplace in the library, some nondescript ones in odd and unexpected corners. The McCullys and the cats coexisted with the understanding that people were people and cats were cats and it was neither possible nor desirable for it to be otherwise. This understanding made for mutual enjoyment. And the McCullys, keeping to their side of the bargain, never gave the cats names—except for the Angora, who had been named Dora. No one knew how this came about and everyone was slightly uneasy at this breach of etiquette.

The parrot, who slept in his cage in the breakfast room, was not yet there. He was still upstairs in bed with Nora. Nora insisted upon this and the parrot, whose disposition was anything but agreeable, permitted this indignity. The parrot bit everyone but Nora, and Helen was convinced it was because Nora had curls.

As usual, the doctor was at his club, the Marshlands. Dr. McCully went to his club as often as possible, every evening after dinner and every Saturday and Sunday afternoon. The Marshlands, otherwise a quite nice club, was for men only; women were not allowed except at the annual ball. The doctor went there to play billiards and bridge. He enjoyed bridge although he played very badly, and since Mrs. McCully was a crack player, the Marshlands was a peaceful solution to that problem.

Mrs. McCully could hear herself think at last. She was alone in the library, except for Max and the black cat, doing hems on cup towels she had ordered from Coulson's agent, Coulson's being in England and the agent coming to Amherst once a year.

Living in Amherst made shopping a game of chance. Amherst had stores such as Barry D. Bent's, the grocer, where the first thing one came upon were the glass cases filled with candies, the glass dishes heaped with Moir's chocolate peppermints and Scotch kisses and taffy, and where the McCullys bought sugar and flour by the barrel; and Mr. Pugsley's dry goods store; and the Amherst Boot & Shoe, owned by Mr. Quigley, where the family shopped for Susan, who never shopped for herself, bringing home her plain black-tied shoes year in and year out.

But Amherst was not the place to find just the right thing to go over pink charmeuse for the evening gown to be worn to the Marshlands ball. For that, one wrote to Isla Fawcett, who was spending the year in England. Isla, the daughter of Mrs. McCully's sister Vess, was a handsome young redhead noted for her great style.

It was a game of chance: one wrote—sometimes there was considerable correspondence about one purchase, sometimes not—and one waited for the wheel to stop to see whether one had won or lost.

Everyone waited. The children nagged: "Where's the package from Cousin Isla?" "Silly, Cousin Isla's too busy having tea at Buckingham Palace with Her Majesty, the Queen, to shop for our mother, isn't she, Mother?" Oh, when is it coming, when is it coming ...?

At last it arrived, smelling miraculously of London fog and Claridge's and the British Museum and Fortnum and Mason's and incidentally of the ship's hold, and everyone gathered round for the grand opening.

This time they had won: Cousin Isla had sent a perfectly lovely tunic of gray net with steel bead embroidery, just the thing to put over pink charmeuse. Mrs. Turner, who was a real dressmaker, would make the dress. Not Mrs. Black, who lived in Sackville some ten miles away, and came twice a year to mend the McCullys up. Mrs. Black always came in every morning on the first train and went home every night on the accommodation at eleven o'clock because the McCully beds were either too hard or too soft and their breakfast tea was too strong or too weak. Mrs. Black was a fuss-budget.

Along with the tunic, Cousin Isla had sent gray silk stockings and gray gloves and a hair ornament, a tiny tortoise-shell comb studded with paste, which she had picked up in a grimy little shop on Portobelto Road and had scrubbed properly. Everyone ooh-ed and aah-ed except Dr. McCully, who no doubt was thinking of the cheque Mrs. McCully would have to send to Cousin Isla.

Mrs. McCully also wanted a fan and for this she wrote to her sister Alice who lived in St. John, New Brunswick: "I would like a little fan, something more to carry than use. Nothing too expensive. I think I would like gray as my gloves are that color...." Alice shopped a great deal for the McCullys—fans and dresses and tags and seals and candles for Christmas, and candy sticks and slippers: "Your resources are never at an end...." Mrs. McCully wrote to her.

But surely Alice should not be asked to produce a pony.

Hot Fawcett was the one for that. Hot was her sister Vess's husband Horace (it was a time when people went in for nicknames, the more outrageous the better) and the father of Isla. Hot Fawcett knew all about horses and loved them so much that he refused to learn to drive a motor car, ever. Hot had picked Mrs. McCully's own driving mare, Gyp, a stylish and gentle creature whose gait was just a little bit like a hackney's, slightly prancing, and whom the McCully children had been allowed to drive from the time they could hold a rein in the hands. And, of course, Hot had picked Vess's handsome Lucille, a true hackney whose arched neck, shining coat, and high-stepping graceful gait made Vess's turnout one of Sackville's sights.

Mrs. McCully was about to put down the cup towel and call Hot right then and there, when she heard footsteps coming toward the library.

It was Susan. Susan had known Mrs. McCully from the time she was born, but ever since she had married "the doctor," as Susan always called Dr. McCully, she was always "Mrs. McCully," never "Miss Ethel" or any of that nonsense. Although Susan had kin in Baie Verte and every summer went to visit them, it was the McCully house that was her home, the place where she wished to die; the McCullys were her family.

Susan Crue was a tiny woman made larger by the severity of her expression. Susan's morning uniform was a black skirt, white blouse, and white apron; in the afternoon, she changed her blouse and put a pin on. She wore a fuzzy wig that looked like a busby and that didn't help matters. But if one took a second look, waiting there in Susan's plain face was a surprise—lovely violet eyes.

"I was wondering whether the doctor would care for jumpers tomorrow," Susan said.

In this instance, jumpers were not sailors' blouses or girls' dresses or coasting sleds, but a kind of molasses cookie that Susan, an excellent plain cook, frequently baked.

Deciding what the doctor would or would not care to eat was a strong bond between Mrs. McCully and Susan. They also had their private jokes on the subject. Such as the turkey soup joke: Susan always made soup from the turkey carcass, the doctor always devoured it, and always insisted that nonsense, they couldn't fool him, that delicious soup was no leftover. There was no such thing as a delicious leftover; all leftovers were inedible. The doctor was quite emotional about leftovers.

But that night, Mrs. McCully wanted to talk about ponies, not jumpers. She told Susan about her plan, down to the last detail, the surprise ending.

Susan, giving Mrs. McCully her full attention, listened without changing her expression.

"Well ...?" Mrs. McCully was waiting for Susan to say something.

But Susan was thinking hard. Finally she said:

"It won't work."

"What do you mean, it won't work?"

"It won't work. You can't keep a thing like that a secret. Someone's bound to talk. I know people."

And Susan did. As it has been said of Socrates that, sitting on the steps of the temple in Athens, he knew more about the world than Alexander conquering it, so it was said of Susan that, standing in her kitchen, she knew more about people than most of those who went out into society.

"Nonsense!" Mrs. McCully retorted with some bravado.

"You mark my words. There are some mean people in this world, even in this town."

And she went up to bed, the matter of jumpers having been left undecided.

And Mrs. McCully went to the wall phone in the hall and called Hot Fawcett.

Hot himself answered.

Mrs. McCully came to the point quickly: "Hot, I want a pony for Christmas...."

"Really, Ethel! What for?"

Perhaps as a result of Susan's prophecy, Mrs. McCully only imagined that she heard the sound of a giggle or two on the line between Amherst and Sackville. But it was true that for some, the nights—and the days, too—were rather lonely, and while everyone knew his own ring, one could make a mistake, couldn't one? And if one did pick up the phone on the wrong ring, one still had to listen to make sure, didn't one?

"If anyone in Amherst so much as mentions the word pony out loud, I swear I'll ..." Mrs. McCully said menacingly.

There was dead silence and then indeed there was a faint click or two.

"The day may very well come," said Mrs. McCully, "when we will regret some of these inventions."

"About the pony ..." Hot said. Hot could talk horses morning, noon, and night.

"Oh, yes, the pony. Well, you'll be happy to hear that I've decided every child should have one."

"In which case you want three?"

Hot was handsome, charming, and a tease.

"One beauty, just one beauty for the children for Christmas."

"I do like a woman who knows what she wants."

"Well, then ...?"

"Well—it just so happens that I am planning to go to Montreal...."

"I knew I could count on you, Hot. And, Hot ..."

"I'm listening."

"Hot, I have such a heavenly idea."

"I'm still listening."

"No, I'm not going to tell. It's going to be a surprise."

"If I know you, Ethel, I'll bet it will be. But I would like to ask you a question."

"Yes?"

"Let's say I find the pony, how the devil are you going to hide it from the children until Christmas?"

Mrs. McCully hadn't figured that one out.

Yet.

Chapter Four

In those days, before jets and all that outer space, when one did one's traveling over the surface of the earth rather than above it, when an overnight trip was a journey, when a journey was an adventure, Montreal was a long way from Amherst. Particularly for a locomotive pulling freight up along the St. Lawrence River, past Montmagny and Rivière du Loup and Trois Pistoles, curving here and there, depositing this and that, rattling through Rimouski, taking on water at Campbellton in northern New Brunswick.

At Campbellton, the locomotive wasn't all that took on water.

Three boys hanging around the water tank heard a faint whinnying from one of the cars. They went to investigate. A coal-black pony regarded them with large black shining eyes, lonely eyes, and frightened, too.

One boy whistled. One said, "Gee!" And the third said, "I'd like to be getting him." They agreed that that would be just dandy.

The pony whinnied again.

"He's thirsty."

"And hungry."

They watered the pony and fed him. He had been thirsty and hungry and, grateful for the attention, allowed the boys to pet him; even nuzzled one.

"Whoever's getting him is pretty lucky, all right."

"I'll say."

"You bet."

"I've got an idea."

"Always bragging."

"Well, I have. Anyone got a piece of paper?"

No one had. But they rummaged around and tore off a scrap from a package that was riding along with the pony in the boxcar.

"Who's got a pencil?"

One boy had a stub.

"Write what I say," said the one who had the idea.

The boy with the stub wrote it down.

"Now we sign our names."

They did, the three of them.

"I've got another idea."

"Gee whiz, two ideas in one day?"

"Write P.S. and say ..."

The boy had to squeeze it in, down in the corner of the ragged piece of paper.

"Now we fasten it to the blanket."

"With what?"

The locomotive was getting up steam.

"With what?"

The train shivered. In the nick of time, the boy who had the pencil remembered he had a pin under his lapel, one he had picked up for good luck. They pinned the note to the pony's blanket, each one gave him a pat, and they jumped off.

They stood there watching the train go off toward Dalhousie, waved to the man on the caboose, who waved back, watched till the train disappeared in the distance.

"Anyone got any idea where Amherst is?"

No one had, not even the boy with all the ideas.

Chapter Five

The first snow was falling in Amherst. And high up in the sky, their necks stretched out as if yearning for the distant sun, a flock of Canada geese were flying south; following their leader in perfect V-formation, in the vast loneliness of the sky they were the very symbol of solidarity.

And walking down the road, coming home from school, Richard and Helen and Nora, walking in that order, were as separated as they could be—by yards and by years—thinking separate thoughts, feeling separate feelings, dreaming separate dreams.

It was late afternoon and in this first light snow the pale yellow house appeared to be floating through the drifting snowflakes.

Suddenly, together they turned their heads toward it, the house where they would now begin to spend their winter afternoons and nights, close to the fires.

The first snow falling lightly was like a scrim curtain across a proscenium; behind it would be the deep winter scene of Nova Scotia. Then the snow would be deep, deeper than a child was tall, reaching past the windows of the first floor, reaching up almost to the roof of the woodhouse. Then they would be snowed in, unable to get out until they dug themselves out. Then out would come the sleds and the bobsleds and the horse-drawn pungs. And the snowshoes. The McCullys, along with the rest of Amherst, would go about their business, clumping over the snow on snowshoes like so many penguins. And they went about their pleasure on them, too. It was a common sight to see children going off to parties on snowshoes, carrying their party clothes in bags.

Then it would begin to be Christmastime.

As if it were inevitable, like a law of nature, Helen remembered her fight with Emma. Remembering, she scuffed a foot through the light snow and remembered her splinter of doubt. Then, not caring whether she bumped into anything or not, she screwed her eyes tight shut and willed herself never to have any more doubts about Santa Claus ever again as long as she lived, not even a splinter of one.

Not even knowing that she was doing so, she began to hum, "Deck the hall with boughs of holly ..."

Nora heard her humming and piped up: "Tra la la la *la*, la la ... la..."

"*La*!" Helen instructed.

Richard turned around. Girls were always singing. But without knowing it, he too began to hum to himself.

"... Troll the ancient Yuletide carol ..."

They walked on, still yards apart, until they came to the woodhouse. There, they stamped the snow off their shoes and their coats and their gloves.

Then they went in. Now, together they had one thing on their minds: food.

No one was in the kitchen. A meat pie was ready for the oven, one of Susan's marvels.

And a plate of doughnuts. They each took one. Richard was the first to pass judgment. "A sinker," he said. "A thinker," Nora echoed.

"Lead," Helen concurred.

Susan, whose puff pastry was always worthy of a master French chef, sometimes made light doughnuts and sometimes made heavy ones. No one knew why, least of all Susan. These were exceptionally heavy.

So the hunt was on.

If Susan wanted you to eat doughnuts, heavy ones included, she did not want you to eat cake. In fact, even if she didn't have doughnuts, she sometimes didn't want you to eat cake.

To find the cake that Susan didn't want you to eat was no easy matter; one needed extra senses or a dowsing rod. Sometimes it was hopeless; at such times, particularly if it was night, everyone was convinced that Susan had taken the cake upstairs to bed with her.

The children hurried, any minute Susan would be back in her kitchen.

They began in the dining room, a room large enough to hold two sideboards. They searched drawers, cupboards, teapots, sugar bowls, the cellarette. They were experts at searching for cake and their fingers moved as lightly and rapidly as Jimmy Valentine's. Even Nora was pretty good. But they had one terrible moment. Helen almost dropped the lid of Grandfather Lowerison's Wedgwood tureen.

Richard caught his breath. "Holy mackerel!" he whispered.

They heard footsteps and scurried back into the kitchen.

Annie, coming from the woodhouse carrying logs, looked at them suspiciously.

"Where's Laurent?" Helen, having already learned that the best defense is an offense, felt very clever. Laurent was the one to attend to the fires, not Annie.

Annie shrugged.

"Where's my mother?" Nora asked, still at the stage where

everything and everyone either belonged to her or didn't exist.

Again Annie shrugged.

"Cat's got her tongue," Helen said.

"Which cat?" Nora asked.

Much to Annie's relief, Susan joined them and now it was her turn to be evasive. She too shrugged and, looking down at the plate of doughnuts, suggested that they each help themselves to one more: Susan could subtract faster than most people could add.

"We'd rather have cake, thank you very much," Nora said sweetly.

Susan's jaw went out and she pointed a stubborn finger at the doughnuts. Knowing when they were defeated, the children each took another doughnut.

"But where are they—my mother and Laurent?" Nora insisted.

"On a mysterious mission, silly...." Helen left the kitchen with her nose in the air.

They were in the living room, sitting, kneeling, sprawling on the floor next to the fireplace where some apple wood was sending up spice-scented smoke.

"What's mysterious?" Nora, who was stuffing a doll into a dress obviously too small for it, wanted to know.

"What no one knows anything about," Helen informed her.

"And is busting to know," Richard said, nodding his head toward Helen.

"Busting is vulgar. But you're busting just as much as I am, Richard McCully, so don't put on any airs."

"I'm busting too," Nora said, determined to keep up no matter what the cost.

"And what are you bursting about?" Grandmother McCully wished to know as she stood in the doorway.

"We don't know, do we?" Nora asked her brother and sister.

Picking up their homework hastily, Helen and Richard became very studious and paid no attention to her.

"Surely you children—" their grandmother began sternly.

At that moment, the snow not yet being heavy enough on the ground, there was the clop clop of a horse's hoofs. The children dropped their books—and doll—and ran to the window.

"—ought not to be bursting over nothing at this time of day when there is work to be done. The devil finds work for idle hands—"

Behind the curtain of falling snow, they saw Gyp coming up the road pulling the carriage (which would not be used again till the snow was off the ground). It was a pretty sight, almost dreamlike. They watched her turn into the lane, and as if she knew exactly where to go in the snow, she pulled up at the front door instead of going directly to the carriage house.

Mrs. McCully handed the reins to Laurent and climbed down.

The children raced to the door.

Mrs. McCully came in with a pink nose, her little fur hat wet from the snow, and looking as if she too were busting with something.

"Where've you and Laurent been?"

"What'd you do?"

"Why's your hat wet?"

"She's not talking." That was Richard.

"Mother's not talking." That was Mother.

"It isn't polite to talk about someone in the third person in her presence." That was Helen reciting a rule she wasn't the least bit interested in.

"Ooh—a present." That was Nora.

"She thinks she's so smart." Richard hated it when Helen—or anyone else for that matter—recited rules.

Mrs. McCully clapped her hands together smartly, making a businesslike noise: "Oh, do stop your babbling, the lot of you, or—"

"Or we'll see stars?" Nora asked.

"Yes," Mrs. McCully said, sounding as if she meant it.

Nora could make herself sneeze and did so. "I've got a cold ...?" she asked somewhat hopefully.

"Nonsense!" Mrs. McCully said. "You have no such thing."

Mrs. McCully did not believe in her children's being sick and consequently they very rarely were. And when they were, they were never allowed to be very sick. Being sick was for people who had nothing better to do.

"Here"—she took off her hat and handed it to Helen. "Shake it out." Then to Richard, "Do give me a hand with these boots, won't you?"

The telephone rang.

"Su-san!" Mrs. McCully shouted.

Susan was afraid of the telephone, and when she was forced to use it, her personality changed; she put on airs: "Miss Helen is not at home," she would say to one of Helen's little school friends who would promptly get the giggles. Or "May I *ahsk* who is calling?" she would ask, if the call was for one of the grownups.

Smoothing her wig as if the person on the other end could see her, she answered the phone. Even from the other end of the hall, they could tell by the look of her that she was being uppity.

Then, in her ordinary everyday voice, she called out: "It's Mr. Fawcett." On her way back to the kitchen, still calling loudly, she asked, "Is he coming to dinner?"

But Mrs. McCully flew down the hall to the telephone without answering.

The children stood where they were, watching her.

Just before she picked up the telephone, Mrs. McCully looked down the hall at her children and shouted, "Go back to doing ..."

Reasonably enough, the children waited.

"What are you standing there for?" Mrs. McCully's voice was rising ominously.

"For you to finish your sentence," Helen spoke for the three of them.

Mrs. McCully took a step toward them.

They started on their way back to the living room.

"Can't you walk a little faster ...?"

" 'Said the whiting to the snail ...' " Helen muttered.

Mrs. McCully took another step toward them and they ran.

"What is she keeping from us?" Helen, who knew her mother well, asked Richard.

"Search me ..."

That was the day the pony arrived in Amherst.

Off in the distance, up northwest of Amherst, the freight train would be coming slowly down from New Brunswick, coming over the Tantramar Marshes, stirring up some wild duck on its way, and entering Nova Scotia via the bridge that went over the Missaquash River.

The station at Amherst, not too far from another river, the Nappan, which comes from the Indian word *Napan* meaning "a good place to get wigwam poles," was a homely structure. No matter: it had its own attraction—trains, trains coming in and trains going out; not many, perhaps a morning train, an afternoon train, an accommodation, a freight train. In those days, it wasn't just that trains were the best way of getting around (there are some smart people who think they still are), or that a train coming in or going out brought goods and mail and passengers, it was that a train brought news that there was a big wide world outside of your own small one. So there were always people—young and old alike—hanging around the station at traintime. Even with the snow beginning to fall.

"She coming in on time?"

"Three minutes late, I hear."

"Tst. Tst."

"Look, someone's pulling up in a carriage."

"Where?"

"There."

"Why, it's Mrs. McCully."

"And their man, Laurent."

"What's she doing here meeting a freight train?"

"Maybe she likes to see a train come in and go out just the same as anybody else."

"Maybe."

Standing off by themselves, looking off into the distance where the train would come from, was a small group of Micmac Indians.

Mrs. McCully and the stationmaster shook hands. The stationmaster knew Mrs. McCully well, all the McCullys in fact. With reason. When the McCullys had to make a train, more often than not it was a close thing. More often than not, someone would have to run to the telephone, call the station and pant, "Hold the train!" And they would. In those days, very likely when the Canadian National Railways made up their schedules for Nova Scotia they allowed for laggards like the McCullys.

"Sure wonder what she's here for."

"Looks to me like she's telling him a secret."

"A good one, too. He likes it."

"He's a funny one, he is. Crossing his heart like a kid."

The train whistle sounded over the marshes.

Mrs. McCully hurried over to the siding where the freight was handled. She was followed by Laurent, the stationmaster, and just about everyone who was hanging around the station, including the Micmacs.

Waiting on the siding to go out were some goods made in Amherst: three coffins, boxes of boots, and some crates labeled "sanitary enamelware," better known as chamber pots.

The train was coming in and there was much slow waving of hands back and forth between the engineer and most people except Mrs. McCully.

The snow was turning her little fur hat white and she had her eyes fixed on a trainman who was walking over the tops of the cars, as the train came in slowly.

Now everyone watched her.

The trainman began to climb down the ladder of a boxcar and Mrs. McCully instinctively ran toward him.

The train stopped.

Mrs. McCully reached the car just as the door was being opened. Laurent and the others caught up with her. They had some trouble opening the door and Mrs. McCully tapped her foot impatiently.

The door was finally opened and a ramp was put down.

"It's a pony!"

Very carefully, Laurent led the pony down the ramp. A ripple, like a shudder, went through the pony's body, and it shook its head and looked out from under its forelock with eyes more frightened than ever.

"What a beauty!"

"That's a big pony all right. No little Shetland pony that one. Around fourteen hands, wouldn't you say?"

Mrs. McCully was smiling and patting the pony and talking to it. In front of everyone, with the snow coming down on the two of them, she rubbed her cheek against its nose.

Then Mrs. McCully gathered her wits. She looked at the people who were murmuring in praise of the pony. She knew this one and that one; she did not know the Micmacs who were waiting for the next train out, no matter which. Now and then a friendly trainman let them ride free, a small privilege for having been dispossessed.

She addressed them all. No one, not one single solitary one of them, was to let her children know that this pony had arrived in Amherst. This pony was to be their Christmas present. Everyone nodded to everyone else. What a lovely idea, every child should have a pony, they assured each other. Or words to that effect. But Mrs. McCully's words were quite explicit. She didn't much care what they said as long as they kept it from her children. Did they promise? They promised—the Micmacs, who were on their way heaven knows where, promising more solemnly than the rest.

Then Mrs. McCully saw the note on the blanket. She took it off and read it in the falling snow. She smiled rather tenderly and put it in her purse. The boys had made one mistake, besides their grammar, but this note was precious and would always be kept, Mrs. McCully decided then and there. (It has been kept and always will be.)

She reached up and brushed the pony's forelock from its eyes; the pony still looked frightened.

Laurent had the bridle in his hand. He was to take the pony to Cody's Stable and Mrs. McCully would meet him there.

On that day, late in the afternoon, quite a few people saw the McCullys' man Laurent walking a beautiful big black pony to Cody's Stable. He went past the Terrace Hotel, Barry Bent's, the post office, the Church of England, the Baptist Church, the Bank of Nova Scotia, and he turned left at Mr. Pugsley's store. Some knew him, some didn't. Those who did were asked, in Laurent's French Canadian accent, to keep their mouths shut. Those who were asked to do so promised they would. A traveler, standing across the road from Pugsley's, wondered what was going on; he put down his sample case and rubbed his chin.

At Cody's Stable a nice stall had been set aside for the pony, and water and oats were waiting for her. Mr. Cody and the stable hands said she was a real beauty, just the kind of pony every child should certainly have. The pony whinnied as if she agreed.

A little weary now, from excitement as much as anything else, Mrs. McCully once again asked everyone to keep her secret, everyone at the stable this time.

By the time Mrs. McCully and Laurent started for home, quite a few people in Amherst, Nova Scotia, had promised to keep it a secret that the McCully children were to get a beautiful black pony with great shining black eyes for Christmas.

The question was: Would they keep their promise? All those people?

Chapter Six

The day came when the McCullys were snowed in for the first time that year. The storm had come during the night, howling and wailing and groaning the way big winter storms do. It blew in over the Bay of Fundy, past the point where Fundy narrowed into Chignecto Bay, through the marshes, blowing up great drifts of snow.

In the country, the caves where the bears were sleeping through the winter disappeared under the snow; the beavers' lodges went under; the little flying squirrels, visible only to people who prowled outdoors at night, peered out from their nests with oversized bright eyes and did no gliding that night.

Seen on a map, Nova Scotia looks like a lobster. That night the lobster lay under snow from Yarmouth down at its tail, to Cape St. Lawrence up north at the tip of the claw.

Laurent, awake at four o'clock in the morning as usual, could not get out the back door of his little house without shoveling his way through the drift. As it turned out, he had to shovel all the way from there to the big house. What with the wind and the blinding snow, it took him a long time to get to the big house; a more fragile man might not have made it. This was one of the big storms and he wished that somehow he had made his way to the barn, too.

That day with the snow piled up outside, with the storm petering out in the late morning and the sun coming out to flood the blue-white snow with pale gold beams, that day became the official opening of the Christmas season in the McCully house.

In the weeks preceding this day, the children had forgotten all about their mother's mysterious mission. They had, jointly and separately, had other things on their minds.

Helen's, by all standards, was the most serious.

It was Emma again. By mutual consent, they had dropped the subject of Santa Claus, but one day on the way home from school they did get around to wishing Christmas would hurry up and come.

"I just can't wait," Helen had said, for about the third time. Emma had said it more than once herself.

"Well, you just better had, because—" And Emma stopped and looked at Helen with a very peculiar look.

"Because why?"

Emma hesitated.

"Because nothing. Because it's a big secret."

In the normal course of events, Helen might very well have tried to extract a big secret from Emma, but if it was about Santa Claus again she didn't want to hear it.

So that dangerous moment passed. But Emma herself could not have said whether or not it had passed for good.

As for Helen, the incident provoked a new worry.

Weighing the evidence, which she did when she should have been doing her homework, she was convinced that nothing more that Emma could have said about Santa Claus could have shaken her belief in his existence. She, Helen McCully, did believe in Santa Claus. What worried her was what he would think of her for having had even one minute's doubt; that is, if he knew about it, which she sincerely hoped he did not.

That worry lasted right through dinner, and when she went to bed that night, Helen squished herself into a little ball, making herself as inconspicuous as possible.

And one day Richard had found the barn door locked.

The barn door was never locked, morning, noon, or night, winter, summer, spring, or fall.

If anyone wanted to play hide and seek, or see a swallow's nest, or climb up into the loft just for the sake of climbing something, the door to the barn was always open.

And now it had been locked and no key in sight.

Richard went storming into the kitchen.

"Who the heck locked the door to the barn?" he demanded of Susan.

"Don't ask me." Susan clamped her mouth shut and made herself very busy washing a cup and saucer she had just finished drying.

"Nor me," Annie said before she had even been asked, and she disappeared into the woodhouse.

He found his mother at her desk, writing a letter to her sister Alice in St. John. "—English bred, with a shining black coat—" she had just written, and jumped as if she had been frightened out of her wits by Richard.

"Goodness, Richard! I didn't hear you."

Richard, who knew he had come in about as quietly as an enraged elephant thundering through the jungle, didn't feel like arguing that point.

"Why's the barn door locked?"

Mrs. McCully folded the unfinished letter in half, making sure it was perfectly even at the edges.

Richard repeated the question.

Mrs. McCully decided to fold the letter into quarters.

"I do think a person ought to be allowed to write a letter to her sister in peace and quiet—"

"Jumping jeepers, it's only a simple question."

Mrs. McCully stared at the letter; what if she folded it into eighths ...?

"Our barn is always open," Richard persisted.

Mrs. McCully swung around in her chair.

"Precisely!" she said. "And what this family needs is a little change now and then. We don't want to get all set in our ways, do we, Richard?"

"But ..."

"But nothing. Tell me something, Richard—" Mrs. McCully looked around the room, up at the ceiling, and down at the floor— "tell me—how's the hockey going?"

Later, when Mrs. McCully told about this, she said it had been a very close call; her mind had gone completely blank; she couldn't think of one reason, except the real one, why that barn should have been locked. Hadn't it been clever of her to distract Richard with hockey? "Clever, my eye," Richard had retorted. "I thought to myself, 'What's she folding that letter all up for as if she were going to send it out to sea in a bottle?'"

But this conversation took place much, much later.

🌿

The day they were snowed in they began to prepare the plum puddings and the fruit cakes for Christmas and the mincemeat for the whole winter.

While Laurent and Richard worked with shovels outside, trying to clear a path, Mrs. McCully and Helen, with some assistance from Nora, began cutting up nuts and picking over raisins. Sitting around the table in the breakfast room, with Max and the parrot and Dora and the other cats waiting for something to fall on the floor, they cracked walnuts, "pigtoes," which were really only Brazil nuts, and almonds.

" 'Tis the season to be jolly ...' " This time Helen knew perfectly well she was singing, and sometimes Mrs. McCully hummed along with her. (In those days, mothers were allowed to sing in the presence of their children without being hushed.)

By evening there were mounds and mounds of nuts and raisins and Laurent had cleared a narrow path, like a tunnel, from the front door to the road.

And that night, caught up in the Christmas spirit, Helen went to bed without a doubt or worry on her mind, stretched out in her normal position.

❧

That night, the house was at rest in a sea of silent snow. The road not having been opened yet, there was not even the sound of sleigh bells.

In the silence, the children, who would be dreaming of Christmas before they had even fallen asleep, did not hear the fall of a man's snowshoes as he made his way to the barn door.

That night the snow silenced everything.

Chapter Seven

Down at the barn, the door remained locked. Except at night. Moving furtively over the snow, Laurent would look up at the big house to make certain no small figures were at the windows, that the children were safely in bed. Then, only then, he would open the barn door, holding his breath for fear it would creak too loudly, and go about his secret, nocturnal task. Each night after he had once again bolted the door, he would let out a big sigh of relief: this night the secret had been kept. But what about tomorrow night?

"What do you mean they locked the barn door?"

"I mean what I say, they did."

"I wouldn't have done that if I'd been them."

"Why not?"

"Kids are bound to get suspicious, bound to."

"Seems to me like the kids are bound to find out some way or other. Whole town in on a secret? It'll be a miracle if someone doesn't spill the beans, a miracle."

"Well, this is the season for miracles, isn't it?"

"Is it?"

The Micmacs, with their fine sense of ceremony and ritual, knew exactly when to come to the McCully house to sell their baskets. Each year they came, the whole family—father, mother, grandmother, and four children—two weeks before Christmas, each loaded down with baskets.

By that time, Mrs. McCully would have made up her list, decided who was to receive baskets this year: the rector and his family, of course; some former servants; some friends—and some strangers, too—perennially or currently on their uppers.

The Indians came with their very best baskets and everyone took part in the selection, including the youngest Indian child. When the transaction was concluded everyone bowed to everyone else and the children were given little bags of candy and cookies and the grownups a glass of wine and some cake. "Merry Christmas, Merry Christmas." The greeting may have been premature, but it is possible that in the warm kitchen of the McCully house some ancient wounds were eased—for that small space of time at least.

Then the Indians would depart, promising to return the next year. But that particular year, as they disappeared past the barn, Mrs. McCully could have sworn that they paused there for a second and that, one and all, they turned their heads toward it. For that second, she held her breath: Would they become too inquisitive? Would they by some sign or sound betray the secret? But, with one last glance at the barn, they went on their way. They were accustomed to secrets.

And just about this time, the ships nosing their way into the cold gray waters of Halifax Harbor, after stormy voyages from Southampton, England, and Le Havre, France, carried in their holds packages of various shapes and sizes addressed to Miss Nora

McCully and Miss Helen McCully and Master Richard McCully and to their parents and grandmother and to Miss Susan Crue, and all were sternly labeled Not To Be Opened Until Christmas! Isla Fawcett, who remembered everyone back home, also indicated on her packages that she wished them to travel on ships named after the royal family—*Royal Edward* or *Royal George* perhaps—and Nell Ryan, a dear friend who had married and gone to live in Paris, would give to the *Florida* or the *Niagara* the privilege of carrying her gifts home.

Every day now Mr. Embree, the postman who delivered mail on his bicycle, and Mr. Dugan, who drove the Express, came with more and more Christmas cards and letters and packages.

The children would race out to them and jostle each other as they grabbed for the privilege of helping to carry the packages in, often shaking one close to an ear, hoping to divine its contents. The ones labeled FRAGILE, Mr. Dugan, jealous of the reputation of the Express, delivered himself to an adult member of the McCully household; handing it over with the utmost delicacy, he would say, "If anyone's going to break it, it won't be me."

And by now, symbolically, as if every man, woman, and child of Amherst had in him the spirit of Christmas, suddenly there were no more red candles to be had in the whole town. And Mrs. McCully wrote to her sister Alice "—Mrs. Calhoun bought pretty corrugated or fluted red candles, with gold bands around the centers at the 5 & 10 store for 5 cents each. Every red candle is gone here. I'm enclosing a dollar for you to buy the worth of it for me. You remember the square mission candles I had last year. These are about the same size, only round and fluted. These if you can get them,"—and again—"there isn't one here."

But there were trees.

Late one afternoon, an afternoon that was disappearing in a mist of flurries, little flurries of snow whirling down from the sky, little flurries of snow spiraling up from the ground, the children watched Laurent drive off with a saw, an ax, and rope beside him. They knew what this was all about: Laurent was going out to the country to the McCullys' woodlot to pick the Christmas tree. And Laurent was a good picker: he always came back with one just the right height, so its top just touched the ceiling, and without any bare holes to hide or camouflage (a word which would not be invented until 1917, during the war).

But, as if its enchantment depended on it, the children never saw the decorated tree until the morning of Christmas.

The nights when the moon was full were the ones to worry about most. A secret could cast a long shadow against the white snow in the light of the full moon. And more than that, as everyone knows, people and creatures get skittish at the time when the moon is full: children turn sharply in bed and sometimes tumble out; a twig snaps for no reason at all—except that the moon is full—and sends a squirrel, a mouse, and a raccoon scampering through the night. An owl takes sudden and unexpected wing in search of a mouse. Unsuccessful, it lets out a hoot.

It frightens a somewhat skittish creature clean out of its wits. This creature lets out its own sound of fright.

Hush!

Now won't a child tumble out of bed?

The creature is hurriedly led away from the light of the full moon.

As if it were at fault.

Bewildered, it wishes it were no longer a secret.

"Wasn't that strange, that again just before Christmas Nora's doll should be broken?" Mrs. McCully wrote to her sister Alice.

The ancients—Druids and such people—would not have thought it strange. It was the winter solstice, the right time for making sacrifices, they would have said.

"But why pick on me? What have I done to deserve a sacrifice?" Nora might well have asked. "Again?"

The year before, on Christmas Eve itself, her favorite doll, a groom doll with a bisque head and bright blue blown-glass eyes, fell and broke his papier-mâché leg. No one knew how. No one had seen a cat or Max or the parrot or anyone else shove him. To almost everyone's horror, he just lay there on Christmas Eve with a broken leg.

Regardless of what Druids and such people would have thought, the doctor and Aunt Alice, who was visiting, spent the better part of Christmas Eve ruining a perfectly good sacrifice by mending the leg until it was quite whole again.

This year the sacrifice happened four days before Christmas, ahead of schedule.

It was a Saturday night and Cousin Leslie had come over from Sackville all by herself on the morning accommodation. Mr. Norton, the conductor, who knew the little boys and girls who occasionally rode the trains alone, and who saw to it that they got off where they should, said good-bye to Leslie at Amherst and cautioned her to be a good little girl because guess who was watching her right now?

"Santa Claus," Leslie replied, looking over her shoulder. It is quite possible that it was this reminder that made her nervous and unsteady on her feet.

After Nora had gone to bed, Leslie and Helen, who were allowed to stay up longer because they were older, decided after much hemming and hawing to play house.

Mrs. McCully and the doctor were about to leave for a party in Tidnish on Northumberland Strait. They were going to make the run out by motor, in those days an event as exciting as the parties themselves. Much depended on the weather, the condition of the roads, and the company and tires. If the company was jolly, it was easier to take the flat tire—which was more than likely to happen—in stride.

That night Mrs. McCully had ascertained that the moon was superb for motoring and that the rest of the company, like herself, were in high spirits.

So the appearance of two little girls with white faces, one tear streaked, at her dressing room door was most unwelcome.

"Whatever is the matter?" she inquired reluctantly, in no mood for the answer.

Neither Helen nor Leslie seemed able to speak and it took some doing to extract the information that Leslie had fallen,

"What's all the fuss about? You don't seem badly hurt," Mrs. McCully said, dabbing her face with powder.

"No, but Gwendolyn is," Helen said.

"And who, may I ask, is Gwendolyn?"

Helen told her.

"Good God, not Gwendolyn!" Mrs. McCully's face paled under the powder.

Gwendolyn was Nora's bride doll, the current pride and joy of her life. Gwendolyn was a flaxen-haired beauty from Dresden, exquisitely dressed in creamy white satin with a wreath of tiny orange blossoms in her tulle veil. Many's the time she had been married, to some king or prince or lord or knight. And once or twice to a nobody. Besides being the most beautiful bride in the world, Gwendolyn had been so willing.

"How badly hurt?" Mrs. McCully asked.

"I'd say she was dead," Helen said. "Wouldn't you, Leslie?"

Leslie burst into tears.

This time the Druids would have been more than satisfied; Gwendolyn was truly beyond repair. China is highly breakable. It was a dreadful sight, a terrible end to a charming bride.

Who was going to tell Nora in the morning?

Leslie said she didn't feel well and wondered whether she couldn't take the accommodation back to Sackville? Please?

Certainly not, she was told.

Why me? Leslie very likely thought. Oh, why did this have to happen to me? And just before Christmas, too?

To which a Druid might have replied: Dear girl, little do you know how lucky you are: in our time, a stranger like you could very well have been the sacrifice.

Wrapped in her furs and veils and with the motor purring nicely, Mrs. McCully settled in for the run out to Tidnish. But when she saw the barn brilliantly lit up by the moon, she had a sudden disturbing thought and said she must have a word with Laurent.

Mrs. McCully told Laurent that because of an unfortunate accident in the big house, two little girls might be restless in the big house that night; she advised him to go about his nocturnal task later than usual.

It was good advice. Two little girls were restless; particularly Helen. Tossing this way and that, Helen couldn't stop herself from thinking about Gwendolyn. Was it possible that the doll's breaking was a warning from Santa Claus? A promise of worse to come?

That night Helen had an awful nightmare: she dreamed that because she had once had that splinter of doubt, Santa Claus went right past the McCully house. Didn't even stop for Richard or Nora.

That night Helen tumbled out of bed.

Chapter Eight

Monday morning the parrot squawked furiously and as if he would never stop.

"What are they doing to you, my poor little bird?" Nora wailed dramatically, jumping out of bed. Nora had not quite recovered from the tragedy of Gwendolyn.

In the hall, she bumped into Helen, who had spent a good part of Sunday telling herself that, pooh! it was only a silly stupid old nightmare and that she wasn't going to give it another thought.

Richard, who was hanging over the banister, nearly upside down like a bat, was making an announcement: they had closed the doors!

"On my poor wee little bird?"

"The doors are closed?" Helen caught her breath with excitement. Surely that meant that everything was going to be all right. Didn't it? Oh, didn't it, didn't it?

It was two days before Christmas. Every year, two days before Christmas the doors to the Big Rooms and the dining room were closed tight and were not to be opened until Christmas morning. To the children, it was always as if a stage were being set behind those closed doors and when at last they were opened, the play would begin.

The children now began a two-day siege compounded of excitement, fidgets, and the need to be on their best behavior or Santa Claus might have some second thoughts. Deep down in their hearts, the children believed that Santa Claus was a loyal, generous friend who accepted the good with the bad, but they were leery of making a test case of it. (Needless to say, Helen with her worry was considerably more leery than the other two.) Occasionally, they were so excessively well mannered that they unnerved the grownups. "Oh, Grandmother," one of them would say, "do sit down and let me bring you a cup of tea." Excessive, it served only to convince Grandmother that she was not being told the truth about her health.

That Monday morning Mrs. McCully thought she had everything well organized and under control: she and Annie would begin to work behind the closed doors of the Big Rooms and the dining room, and Helen would be put to work in the breakfast room wrapping Christmas gifts that were to be delivered by hand.

Everything was under control until Laurent made an error in judgment.

Helen had left the breakfast room and was on her way to the library for some glue to help make a decent-looking package out of a Toby jug, when she saw Laurent on his way to the Big Rooms carrying what looked like a large rolled-up rug. Helen, preoccupied as she was with the task ahead, this Toby being an unusually fat fellow, most likely would have paid no attention to Laurent if he hadn't acted so suspiciously. Seeing Helen, he turned back and came as close to tiptoeing away as a man could who was carrying such a large bundle.

"Laurent!" Helen called. "What've you got there?"

Laurent lost his head and tried to run.

"Laurent!"

Burdened as he was, he couldn't run, but he wobbled as fast as he could down the hall and out into the kitchen.

Helen went after him and had the kitchen door slammed in her face by Annie.

At this point, Helen forgot that she didn't really want to know what was going on behind the closed doors before Christmas, that she really wanted to be surprised. But all this was too much for her and she banged on the door just as Susan was about to separate an egg.

The egg was separated—but on the floor.

As everyone knows, life in a large family is apt to be filled with hullabaloos that lean toward slapstick.

The loss of the egg hit Susan in three sensitive spots; her vanity—she fancied that with her skill she ought to be able to separate an egg during an earthquake; her thrift; and her pride in her kitchen floor.

In the midst of this, old Mrs. McCully discovered that there was to be a rum punch on the Christmas menu. Were it not for the hullabaloo, she would have been attending to her morning mail. Old Mrs. McCully having regarded the bottle of rum as if her nose were being assaulted by some very old fish, young Mrs. McCully tried to hide the brandy for the brandy sauce and the claret for the claret sauce. However, she whisked rather too energetically and to the loss of one egg was now added one good bottle of claret.

Helen maintained that she was an innocent bystander and moreover that she ought to be complimented on her good manners for knocking on a door before entering.

There was one good thing to be said for that particular

hullabaloo: not one of them heard the sudden, unexpected sound from the barn.

But the boy who had just delivered five pounds of butter from Barry D. Bent's grocery store had heard it. These were busy days at Barry Bent's, and when the boy returned to the store it was crowded with people shopping for Christmas.

"I heard it, down at the barn at the McCullys'," the boy said, "loud as all get out."

"In broad daylight?"

"It doesn't know it's a secret."

"I don't believe it is."

"Don't believe it is what?"

"A secret. You mean to tell me you believe those kids don't know all about it? You can't keep a thing like that a secret. Not on your life, you can't."

The person who said this was a notorious gossip with a mean disposition.

There was a slight movement toward this person.

"Maybe you can't keep a secret," someone said breathing hard.

The gossip took one step back in the direction of the exit.

"Maybe he hasn't kept it a secret ..."

"Maybe he hasn't ...?"

The gossip retreated another step.

"Maybe I haven't...." The gossip was smiling meanly.

A lady who had remained at the counter trying to decide between two different kinds of biscuits looked up and, seeing the gossip's mean smile, said absent-mindedly: "Scrooge!"

She wasn't the only one who made the connection: everyone who was Christmas shopping that morning in Barry Bent's was reminded of Scrooge.

Looking meaner than ever, the gossip stamped out of the store.

But no one knew whether he had or had not or whether he would or would not spoil the secret. They only knew he was the meanest man in town.

When the evening star appeared over the marsh, Helen asked: "Now is it Christmas Eve?"

Richard, who was carrying the last basket from the kitchen, stopped and waited for the answer. Since this basket was for the rector and his family, it was by far the heaviest—a large turkey and fixings, plum pudding, fruitcake, jams and fruits rested on a bed of greens, and tucked inside with a note, a cheque. Slightly bent over the weight, Richard stood still with the tip of his tongue touching the tip of his nose.

"Now? Now?" Nora asked sounding like a cat.

Mrs. McCully tied the last bow on the last package, her fingers fluttering.

"Now, yes now, it is Christmas Eve." She spoke slowly, as if she too, like her children, had been waiting and waiting.

"All over the world is it Christmas Eve now?" Helen asked, wondering why her mother sounded so odd.

"Not in China, it isn't." Richard set the basket on the floor next to the other baskets, some filled with ham, some with pork roasts, some with chickens. "Or in Africa."

"Or in Halifax?" Nora inquired.

They heard the sleigh bells, silvery in the cold clear evening. Laurent was bringing the pung around and the children ran for their hats and coats. With Richard at the reins, the children and Laurent were going to deliver the baskets and other gifts.

The back of the pung was piled high with the packages and the baskets, and the children sat on the seat with one buffalo rug under them and another one on top. Gyp whinnied softly and the pung slid off into the night just as the moon came up.

In those days, in that place, people didn't go in much for greening and lighting up the outsides of their houses for Christmas. An occasional candle in a window, a tree or a wreath seen behind a curtain, sometimes a wreath on a door, that was all. With its blanket of snow, with its own spruce and pine, with sleighs and sleigh bells, Amherst had been transformed into a Christmas scene out of a picture post card or an engraving by Currier & Ives.

In one house, a woman who was on the telephone saw the McCully children go by in the pung and told her friend on the other end that it was as pretty a sight as she had ever seen. The friend fancied it must be, but being a worrisome woman, she worried about the children running into the gossip on their rounds. If it had been up to her, she wouldn't have taken any last minute chances; she would have kept those children safe at home. "Oh, no one would be that mean," the first woman said, "not on Christmas Eve."

But the worrisome woman wasn't so sure.

All the stars were out, brilliantly white in the cold northern sky.

Every once in a while, the children heard the bells of another pung before they saw it and when they caught up with it, friend or stranger, they called out to each other: "Merry Christmas! Merry Christmas!"

In and out they rode, slipping over the snow with its night shadows, carrying their gifts.

Sometimes there was a tree to be seen at someone's house. Or a fire to warm themselves at. Or some old rheumatism to be told about. Or a new baby to hold. Once they joined some carolers.

Nothing unusual about it, just the lovely way Christmas Eve always was. But—

They had just delivered a basket to a very old lady who said she was too old to be polite and wished to inspect its contents then and there. She did so, clucking with approval until she poked her fingers into the pork: about the pork, she would reserve judgment.

Then she peered into each child's face, her eyes sharply inquisitive. Then she shook her old head and laughed.

"What's so funny?" Helen asked.

"Tomorrow." And the old lady laughed some more.

What did the old lady mean? Not wanting to know, Helen tugged nervously at Richard's coat for them to leave. The old lady was still laughing when they left.

Back in the pung, they rode silently for a while. Finally, whispering so that neither Laurent nor Nora could hear her, Helen asked Richard whether he thought that everyone, not just the old lady, was looking at them funny tonight. Richard said that girls were always imagining things. Helen said it was a pity that boys never did. But they spoke as friends who happened to hold different views, not crossly. It was Christmas Eve.

The McCully place was blazing with lights—the house, the barn, and the carriage house. Anyone passing by could see figures rushing in and out among the three buildings. Anyone who didn't know might have wondered what was going on and anyone who knew would surely have wondered what they had done about the children.

The children were on their way home.

"What's Christmas cheer?" Nora had asked, but had fallen asleep before she got the answer.

More than once that night, they had been told they had brought some, but the truth was that they were coming home with more than they had given. They were tingling with it, tired as they were, even

Nora who had fallen asleep.

Helen looked north across the marsh, white and strange and silent in the moonlight. She strained her eyes with looking and her ears with listening. Under the best of circumstances, did he ever make a mistake and go right by someone's house she wondered. Did he?

When they passed Morse's Corner and saw their house, Richard pulled the reins in, pretending to fiddle with something.

The house was beautiful.

Their house had been greened. They could see the wreaths in the windows and the frosted bells.

There had never been a more beautiful house and there never would be.

It was worth waking Nora up to see it.

Richard would have headed Gyp back to the carriage house, but Laurent, who had been asleep most of the time, woke up with a start and said no, he would take over.

Milk and cookies were waiting for them in the breakfast room. And many questions: What had this one said? And how had that one looked? And how did so and so feel?

Everyone seemed to be listening with extraordinary attentiveness to their answers and peering at them as if there were something special to see.

"—and everyone was nice to you tonight?" Mrs. McCully asked and could have bitten her tongue. "It just slipped out," she told Dr. McCully later.

The children thought this the most peculiar question they had ever heard: of course everyone was nice; it was the night before Christmas, wasn't it?

On their way up to bed, one by one the children stopped in front of the doors to the Big Rooms. Richard pretended he was going to open the doors and provoked shrieks of protest.

Nora did a silly jig.

And Helen crossed her fingers and said under her breath, "I do believe! I do believe!" And as she went past, looking over her shoulder, she couldn't help adding, "Oh, please, if you are going to pass us by, don't let anyone know it was my fault, will you?"

Chapter Nine

That Christmas morning began as it always did with the blowing of the horn. Coming from the ice-cold darkness outside, waking them up, there would never be a more musical—or a merrier—reveille than the one blown on that horn. For the children, its sound would remain for all time the sound of Christmas: Santa Claus was about to depart and Christmas was about to begin.

Usually they would jump out of bed and race to the hall window overlooking the marsh, and it would always be Helen who was certain she could see his sleigh just rounding an island of spruce on its way back up north.

But that Christmas morning, immediately after the horn blew, something terrifying happened: the whole house shook—the pictures on the walls quivered, the toys on the shelves, the children's beds— and there was also a noise, a very loud rumbling one. At five o'clock in the morning things shake more and sound louder.

Helen was so frightened she jumped out of her bed and right into Nora's. Did this shaking mean that Santa Claus had not left? That he was still there and furious? In the past, Santa Claus had been such a quiet person, neither seen nor heard, and Helen, for one, preferred it that way.

It was Richard with a very pale face who said: "Come on. The horn blew, didn't it? Let's go."

Keeping close together, they tiptoed through the upper hall. The shaking had stopped, and so had the rumbling, but everything felt strange, as if all the grownups had gone away during the night and left the house to the children.

It was exceedingly quiet. The moon and the stars were still out but lights had been turned on. Still keeping close together, they slipped down the stairs and down the hall toward the Big Rooms.

Helen was the one who stopped.

Now she had heard a thump!

Feeling very pale, she asked Richard in a whisper if he had heard anything. Remarkably polite, but whispering himself, he agreed that it was possible that a log had popped. Or something like that.

But when they reached the Big Rooms, there was another thump.

Even Richard heard it; but he was a boy and had to be brave, so he thought. He kept on going, began to open the doors.

But Helen was a girl and she hung back. If Santa Claus was angry and was going away without leaving anything and it was going to be the worst Christmas anyone had ever had and it was all her fault …

She followed Richard in, but she kept her eyes closed.

He stopped so suddenly that she bumped into him and Nora bumped into her.

The thump that was heard then could very well have been Helen's heart.

"Look!" Richard said. "Look!"

It wasn't easy, but Helen opened her eyes.

The children stood still, as if transfixed, each one convinced it was an apparition. For a second, it looked as if they would never move again, as if standing there in the Big Rooms on that Christmas morning they had become for all time a photograph in the McCully family album.

For there, in the Big Rooms, come into their own with a Christmas tree covered with an angel and glowing with many tiny candles, with garlands of spruce over their windows, with wreaths and poinsettias, there in the Big Rooms of all places, along with their stockings and piles of other gifts, gazing at them with eyes as surprised as theirs was a big black pony.

Standing beside the fireplace, looking very large indeed, with a wreath around its neck, it was as unlikely a sight as a child would ever see on a Christmas morning, or any other morning for that matter.

❦

"In your house?" Even the most polite of those who were to hear about it were not quite polite enough to hide their disbelief. "A pony in your house?"

"Well, tell us, tell us, how did it feel to have a pony in your house for Christmas?"

Wonderful. How else?

"And what did you do when you saw a pony in your house for Christmas?"

People ask such ridiculous questions.

❦

When a pony is in your house, you don't scream and jump and carry on for joy. You control yourself. You gather your wits about you and very quietly and quite slowly, one by one, and all together, you go up

to the pony. You rub its nose. If you can reach, you hug it. As usual, Santa Claus had left part of the doughnut. You give it to the pony. The pony nuzzles you, one by one. You still remember, each one of you, the way that felt.

When the pony whinnied, the grownups came out from wherever they had been and everyone talked at once.

"Oh, look what Santa Claus brought us this time! Look! Look!"

Max got in by mistake and seeing a horse in the house quite naturally barked. The pony shied. That was a scary moment. Richard said, "Jeepers, maybe she'll bust the place up." And no one corrected his English.

It was decided that a house was not the place for a pony. The children began to protest, especially Nora, but they quieted down quickly: the pony was about to take its walk. In the Big Rooms it was quite a walk from the fireplace to the verandah. The McCully children would grow up to see a flight into space, which would be very interesting, of course; but the experience was not to be compared with seeing a pony walk through your house on Christmas morning, step daintily on a rug, go past the tip-top table, the lady's chair and the gentleman's chair, the Victorian sofa, flick its tail over the keys of Mrs. McCully's Chickering piano, go past the ottoman, and all that bric-a-brac, making the house shake again, making the crystals on the candelabra tinkle, go past the Christmas tree with its candles, go through the door, out onto the verandah, and down the steps. That was a walk to remember.

And Mrs. McCully, having watched her children while they were watching the pony, was satisfied that her idea had been a good one.

The children were opening their other presents and their stockings when Nora, for apparently no reason at all, went over to the fireplace and peered up the chimney, studying it hard. Helen looked up and saw her. Jumping up from the floor, she went over to Nora and led her away, distracting her with a new toy. Helen felt very grown-up at that moment, the most grown-up she was to feel for a long time, maybe ever. Mrs. McCully had seen this and quickly told the children to come to the carriage house when they were dressed for church.

In the carriage house, the children discovered that when it came to ponies, Mrs. McCully had thought of everything. There they found the pony already hitched to a little bright-red sleigh, complete with buffalo robes. And next to it was a beautiful little basket cart to use when the snow melted. And an English saddle for riding. Everything a child or a pony could want.

The sleigh was just big enough for three children. Everyone who saw them that day had something to remember: the scarlet sleigh with its bells; the faces of the children; and the pony. The pony stepped as if it were very happy not to be a secret any longer.

All of the Fawcetts, except Cousin Isla, came to Christmas dinner that year and the dining room had never looked lovelier. This room too had been greened with garlands of spruce, and like the Big Rooms, its mantel was banked with holly. Dr. McCully had sent Mrs. McCully primroses and azaleas which she had placed here and there. And all around the room were the red candles from St. John, making a ring of flame on the plate rail.

The table had been set with the captain's Wedgwood and the captain's silver, and in the center there was a basket of ferns and white hyacinths.

Everyone always wants to know what everyone else has for Christmas dinner and Mrs. McCully wrote to Alice that her menu was as follows: oyster cocktails, bouillon, shrimp and mushroom rosettes, turkey, cranberries, peas, potatoes, and ham. She also mentioned the fact that old Mrs. McCully had "licked up the rum punch in fine style" along with the plum pudding with brandy sauce and the frozen pudding with claret sauce and whipped cream. Lest anyone go hungry, the menu also included pound cake, nuts and raisins, candies and grapes, bonbons, and coffee. No one went hungry.

The conversation that year was mostly about the pony, who had been named Jenny.

After dinner, when various people had gone off to take naps in various places, Mrs. McCully was alone in the Big Rooms with Richard and Helen, Nora having been one of those who couldn't keep her eyes open.

It was then that Mrs. McCully brought out the ragged piece of paper which had been attached to the pony's blanket and showed it to Richard and Helen:

Dear Friend

    Just a line to let you know we seen your pony in Campbellton N.B. We watered an feed him in the car gave him hay he seems to be very friendly We wish we were the owners

                              Yours truly
                              P.S. drop us a card
                              Earl Lutes
                              Plenery Samon
                              Daniel De War

When they had finished reading the note, Richard and Helen said yes, they would write a card and tell the boys that she had been named Jenny.

Then they were quiet.

"It was nice of those boys to feed Jenny," Helen said thoughtfully after a while.

"Yes, it was," Mrs. McCully agreed.

She, too, became thoughtful as she looked at Helen.

"One might even say," Mrs. McCully continued, "that the spirit of Santa Claus was already on its way that day up there in Campbellton. As far as I can see, all that really matters is the spirit."

By evening the news had spread: the secret had been kept, right up to the last minute.

"To think that a whole town could keep such a secret!"

"Never could have believed it possible."

"Almost feel as if *I* got a pony for Christmas."

"Me, too."

"Rather makes you believe in Santa Claus, doesn't it?"

"I call it a miracle!"

"Well, it's the season for miracles, isn't it?"

"Yes, it is."